*This is the story of two girls, born 250 years apart
—that became best friends.
It's going to sound a little hard to believe, but trust me it happened.
I know because I am one of those girls…*

Rocco

Tara

Ethan

Madeline

Melanie

Izzy

1

Let me introduce myself.

I am Madeline Marie Curry, and when this adventure began I was 8 years old.

Funny, because I don't remember much of my first 7 years—except Mom, Dad, a little bit of school and Uncle Bobby.

At my last physical Dr. Patel told me that I am, at 4'6" a little below average height for my age—but at 70 lbs I'm a little overweight.

Oh well, I am a happy kid any size you wanna call me.

I like to wear jeans and t-shirts and to have my blonde hair braided or in a pony tail.

At school I have a few good friends; Rocco, Ethan, Melanie and Tara. We eat lunch together, and in school the 5 of us are inseparable. But after school, we all go in different directions.

After doing my homework, I could be found reading and looking forward to my next adventure with Uncle Bobby.

Uncle Bobby was a larger than life character, always happy, always trying to help anyone—anywhere.

He took me to my first baseball game at Yankee Stadium, my first concert (Dave Mathews Band), the zoo, the beach and we loved to eat Chinese food together. He even showed me how to use chopsticks!

My Dad, Zack is a computer programmer, and Mom, Angela works at a gift store named Sum Thin Speshel.

Dad, always seemed to be glued to the computer and Mom, being in retail—Her schedule varied from week to week, which left plenty of time to be with Uncle Bobby.

I came to a real appreciation of time a month after my 8th birthday, and for that matter—life itself.

My birthday is July 7. I was born 7/7/07 and this is why so many people think I am such a "lucky" person. Luck, has little to do with a birthday.

You see, on my 8th birthday Mom, Dad, me and Uncle Bobby went out for; You guessed it, CHINESE!

I will never forget that night, or the events that followed shortly after. When we finished our eating and got our fortune cookies, we all opened them up and read them aloud.

Mom's read: Follow the path, but watch out for the trees

Dad's read: Hard work is rewarding

Uncle Bobby's: Appreciate your days

Mine: You will meet a special friend soon

All vague and trite enough I think we all thought, but…

The days that followed my 8th birthday were typical Connecticut July days; hot and humid.

So on Saturday the 16th Uncle Bobby took me to the beach, I remember the sand was so hot, but worth it when I got into the cool Long Island Sound water. We were at the beach a couple of hours and Uncle Bobby brought me home. He would always say *"Love ya Madeline, see ya later!"*

July 16th, he said "Bye Madeline, Love ya!"

Neither of us knew, it was "Good-bye" and I would never see my Uncle Bobby alive again. He was hit and killed instantly by a texting driver.

To say I, or we were devastated is a tremendous understatement. My heart felt like a Piñata. It was unbearable, and every July—I visit his grave and bring a new Yankee cap.

R.I.P. Uncle Bobby

At 8 years old, your mind can't comprehend such matters as death, or life for that matter. Things just are, and we just are.

Except now, Uncle Bobby and our wonderful times together "ARE" no more. He lay there in the coffin, pale and unsmiling. I insisted on seeing him one last time, and although my heart screamed so loud it could have shattered windows, I was only able to whisper "Bye Uncle Bobby, Love ya"

At the cemetery it was worse, and I couldn't believe anything could be, but it was.

All I could think was; all these people were once living, but my Uncle was FULL OF LIFE! And now, he's not.

The minister was praying, as were all the grown-ups there. I couldn't bear any more, so I wandered away looking at the tombstones of people who lived to be so much older than my Uncle Bobby's 33 years.

It was then I came across a very old grave. Something made me stop and read the entire stone, and this is what it reads:

Miss Olyve Stone
Born 1758   Died 1775
Dau of Nathaniel & Mary Stone
Ye Young, Ye Gay
Attend this speaking stone
Think on her fate, and tremble
At your own
For death is a debt to Nature due
Which she has paid, and so must You

At first, I admit I thought it was cool and for a fleeting minute for the first time my mind was not on my beloved Uncle.

And I began to talk to Miss Olyve. I said Miss Olyve it looks like you were taken far too soon too. I hope you didn't suffer. I hope you knew you were loved, and if you would like to come with me—you can.

She did.

Since Uncle Bobby died, Madeline just couldn't sleep and she probably cried 10 gallons of tears.

But, that night, after the events and feelings she experienced—feelings she would never wish on her worst enemy.

Yup, we all know, even when we were 8 years old—there was that *one person* who pushed your buttons.

Nemesis? Enemy? Isabelle Stratton?

One in the same. But, Madeline wouldn't wish any of this on Izzy.

That night, Madeline fell fast asleep. Perhaps her little mind and body knew what she needed most, and well **DING!!! "One order of SLEEP coming up!"** But, apparently it was only a side order of sleep. Because, at 11:06pm her eyes opened and she saw her clock on the night stand—the one Dad said was her "Clutter Station".

But, she also saw her.

What Madeline saw was just as she always heard a ghost would look like. Translucent, fully clad, somewhat hovering.

A woman, no, a teenager—smiling at Madeline.

No deep cold temperatures, no books flying across the room (Madeline LOVED reading about far away places—the cultures, the food, the people).

None of that, just a smile.

They spoke at once. Then they BOTH giggled.

Madeline had waited 10 seconds to speak. Miss Olyve had waited 240 years and it amused her that after waiting all that time, it would be at the precise moment the person she was going to speak to—spoke as well.

Madeline was surprised at herself as well, not to see a ghost. But, to realize there was still a giggle left in her after all her joy in life was buried just that afternoon.

Madeline spoke, uninterrupted at first asking "Are you what I think you are?"

The response washed over her like a warm blanket on a very cold day; *"If ye believes I am a Spirit. Ye are Correct. If ye believes I have evil intent, ye are incorrect. I am Miss Olyve Stone and ye visited my resting place in the Morn. Ye made an offer that resting souls often hear from shallow thrill seekers. Resting souls prefer to rest, rather than be conjured up like some minstrel, then to be exorcised when things do not go the way of the nuisance. Your offer to come with ye, was not taken lightly."*

After a brief pause, Miss Olyve continued

"After conferring with Robert, or as you knew him—Uncle Bobby. We agreed that ye and I should be Friends"

YOU TALKED TO UNCLE BOBBY?!?!

Then, the tears came, like a Colorado river in the Spring.

13

"Yes, Madeline we spoke and he told me to tell ye: If you don't stop crying your head is going to de-hydrate and look like a dried up gourd. Remember our good times Because some people never get to have even one good time.

Miss Olyve continued, *"Grief is natural, as natural as death itself. I penned my own epitath, but the living do not realize that when you remember a passed person, a part of their soul still lives. Your Uncle told me many things about you and asked that I ease your pain and remind you that life and living is so precious.*

When a living person AND a spirit request that you be with Someone on the same day—IT IS TO BE.

That is why I am here and here I will stay until you say four times in a row 'It is Time Miss Olyve, For You To Go'

Now sleep my dear Madeline, sleep well and dream naught for in the morning we shall begin to do a lot.

But, before thou sleepest, perhaps you could think on how to get those Gargoyles out of your yard, they are a troubling bunch."

Those were the last words Madeline heard that night.

Morning came and Madeline's first thought was "was that a dream?" (after having seen A Christmas Carol on Broadway with Uncle Bobby last December).

But, before she even finished that thought she heard "I am not a dream, and you know what to say if you want me to go"

24 Hours, 24 Hours!!! In just 24 hours Madeline felt she had gone from the pits of despair, to making a "Special Friend"

Miss Olyve then said *"We need to follow some simple rules, and there are many. But most important is you cannot tell another living person I exist. They will not be able to see me and it will only create problems. This you must swear to"*

I swear said Madeline.

Miss Olyve continued *"You must never utter such phrases as 'Drop Dead' or 'I wish I were dead' and similar phrases.*

'Tis a great sin to not appreciate life and it angers, insults and hurts spirits. Because so many of them did not understand what a precious gift that was bestowed upon them by the Almighty.

The worst feeling known to spirits is discovering that one loved life
Only after it was over.

As for me, Miss Olyve continued "I shall be your friend and will refrain as I see fit from intervening in your life.

We shall be Friends and travelling partners,
And travel my dear Madeline—we shall"

The Contest? What Contest?

Global Travel Excelsior

You've probably seen their commercials on TV. You know the ones where they Say: **Global Travel Excelsior *No One Takes You Places More!***

Yeah, corny—I thought too. But, they became a trillion dollar company with their Headquarters in Boise, Idaho

Or, you might have heard of their Global—as in world wide campaign they ran this past Spring where one child would win 6 trips to any destinations of their choosing; 1 every six months for 3 years. The child must be 7 to 10 years old, and could bring 2 adults with them.

When I saw those commercials I thought I'd have a better chance at winning the Wonka Chocolate Factory—which is to say, no chance. So, I didn't pay any attention to that contest and was glad when those commercials stopped.

But, like most other kids I thought "How COOL would that be?" Especially with my interests of life in foreign lands.

My Dad said "All they're doing is fattening their data bank to send more e-mails luring people to take vacations they can't afford!"

I knew he was right, but oh Ireland how I would love to see YOU!

And, Thailand, Peru, Greece—THIS WHOLE WONDERFUL PLANET!!!

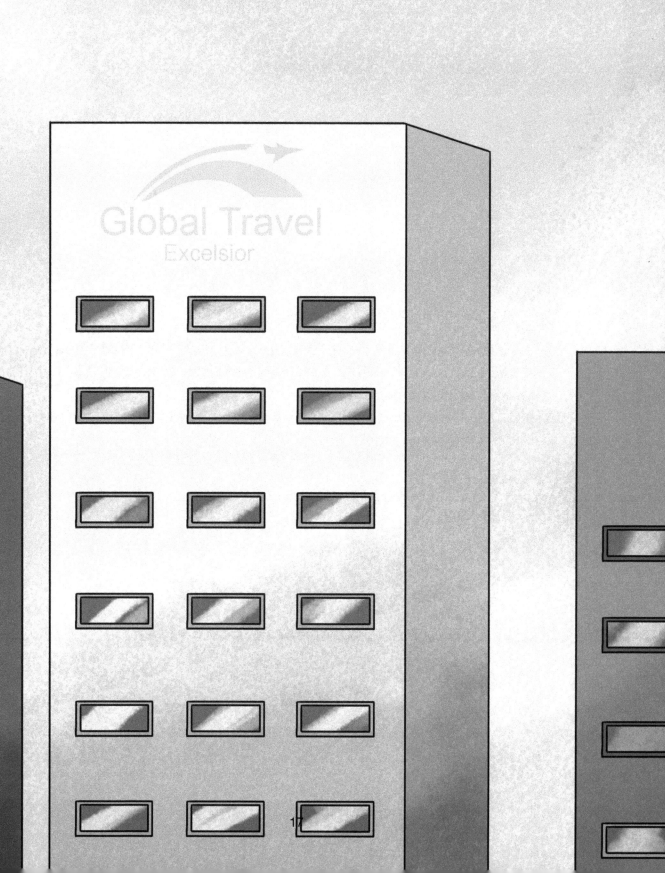

So, even tho it was a 15 on the 1 to 10 COOLOMETER, I knew it was pointless, and I have my books. No batteries or electricity needed. The original Solar Powered entertainment.

Besides that, I had Uncle Bobby and we were having spectacular adventures that would go on forever, right?

About the Fam

Dad and Uncle Bobby were born and raised in Norwalk, Connecticut

The only two children of Gregory and Sarah (Morris) Curry. They lived in an apartment and went to local public schools, and while Dad was a bookworm who took to computers like a fish to water, Uncle Bobby was the adventurer, Cutting school to see the Yankees and Mets whenever he could, while doing enough work at the end of the marking period to pass.

Dad loved school, Uncle Bobby—not so much.

Uncle Bobby would tell me "Madeline I felt like a caged animal—life happens outside, not in a classroom"

Dad would answer him with "The classroom <u>makes</u> your life livable"

Same parents, yet polar opposites.

Dad went to community college and excelled at computers from their infancy thanks to the computer boom of the 1980's and 90's

It was at the community college where my parents first met and it was the proverbial love at first sight!

Mom was from Danbury, Connecticut, the third daughter of Martin (Granpa Marty) and Susan (Williams) Morris. There were no sons and my Aunts moved to California and have a snack shop in San Diego called *Blazin Raisins* where they sell flavored raisins and granola products.

(BTW: their names are Emma and Gloria and they're still single if you guys are interested)

Uncle Bobby, as Dad said more than once " is a man's genius, with a boy's asperations". In that if he went to school he could have written his own ticket. Instead, Uncle Bobby became a "Consultant" and could come into any business, anywhere and create solutions to make that business more profitable, without anyone losing their job.

Amazing man, he was.

I guess you could say the last two amazing things Uncle Bobby did was talked Miss Olyve into being with me on his burial day, and entered my name into **Global Travel Excelsior's Kid's Travel Contest**

Which as I understand, made kids around the world start demanding travelling abroad—their parents succumbing and **Global Travel Excelsior** raking in money like no other company before or since.

Neither my parents or I knew he had done this, and we never would have had a clue I would win.

THAT'S RIGHT!!! I WON!!!

Over 385,000,000 entries, and the person who won didn't even know she was in the running!

I was in shock when they came to our house (Ed McMahon Style I have been told, whoever he was) on August 1st!

There was camera crews, about 150 people all told. Microphones, Local and National News people all to see ME!

It WAS like Willy Wonka's on steroids! Mom actually fainted, but Dad who always seemed to connect the dots mumbled "Thank you Bobby, you're still surprising us".

But how? How does one catch this big of a lightning bolt in a little glass jar? Was there an intervention? Perhaps a little help from beyond?

Whew! I'm Glad That's Over

After a couple of weeks of meeting with people from **Global Travel Excelsior** all the details were explained. Things like Behavioral Clauses and Respect Clauses; Being a good traveler, understanding that *our* culture is different than the rest of the world's. It doesn't make either more right, so be respectful.

Also, to stay out of trouble. Any arrest or law breaking at all would be a rules violation and all future trips would be null and void. So don't do something stupid like shoplift, any place on Earth—got it?

Things finally calmed down, but I had one more jackpot to claim. Seeing Izzy's face when I was at the Shop More, Eat More, Save More Market WAS PRICELESS.

And now it's time for Back to School. I can't begin to say what a tumultuous Summer that was. Too much for an 8 year old, that's for sure. Or, as Uncle Bobby would say "Madeline, sometimes life throws you curve balls and you just gotta go with the pitch". At the time I just nodded, but had no idea what he was talking about. I do now. Well, it feels like Life was pitching curve balls to me all Summer long and now I get to go to school as THE GIRL WHO WON.

I just hope Life starts throwing stuff I can handle real soon. Because, if it weren't for Miss Olyve, I think Madeline would be a lost cause.

People still shout out "Hey! Take ME with ya!" Annoying? Just a lot.

Hey, Miss Olyve—Did you?

During the craziness that was August—I asked Miss Olyve if she was responsible for my winning? Or, was it Uncle Bobby? And she said *"A spirit can request confidentiality from another spirit, and that bond cannot be broken unless there is harm to follow. I might be keeping a secret, but perhaps Madeline, you just won."*

I guess she's right, sometimes when you look a gift horse in the mouth—the horse will bite you.

And I'm so looking forward to Ireland this Christmas Vacation. And, Miss Olyve is going on an airplane.

Or, as Miss Olyve told me:
We shall be friends and travelling partners
and, travel my dear Madeline
we shall…

to be continued after the Ireland vacation

About the Author

R. E. Kensek was born and raised in Norwalk, Connecticut with a love for sports, music, and traveling. Reading about foreign landmarks, foods, and cultures was always a favorite pastime.

Having performed a wide variety of occupations over the years that paid the bills but were unfulfilling, R. E. Kensek now has Miss Olyve and Madeline to write about—the dream job at long last.